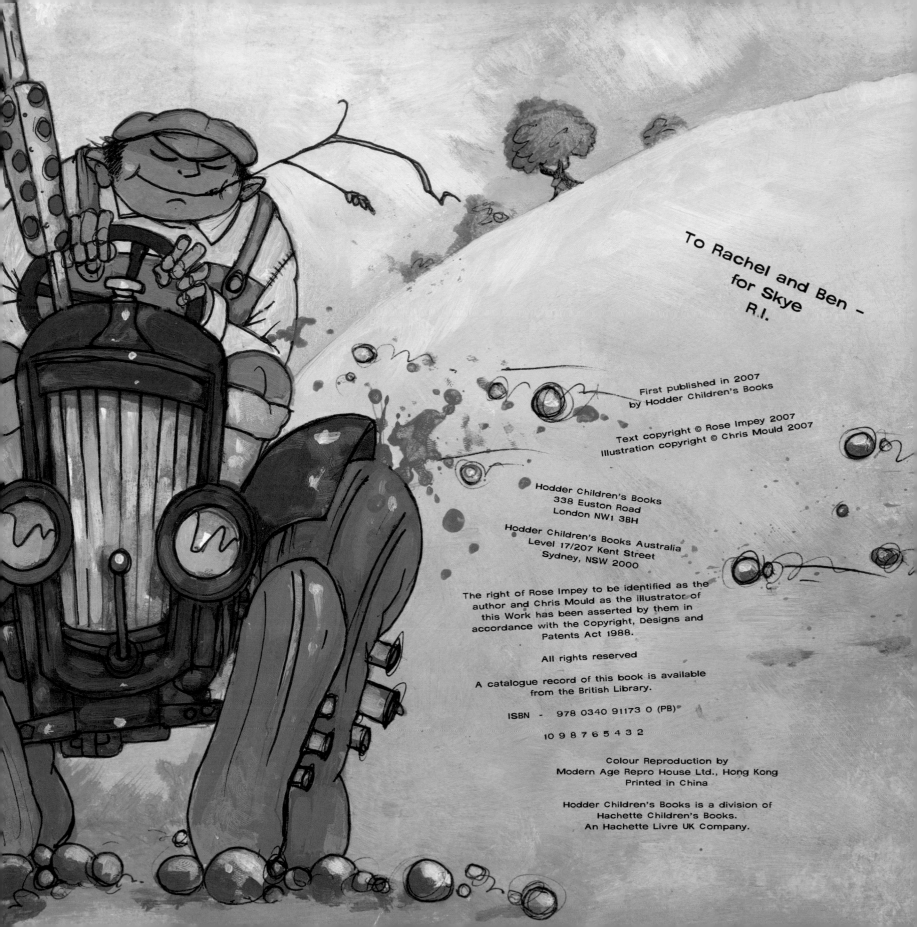

To Rachel and Ben –
for Skye
R.I.

First published in 2007
by Hodder Children's Books

Text copyright © Rose Impey 2007
Illustration copyright © Chris Mould 2007

Hodder Children's Books
338 Euston Road
London NW1 3BH

Hodder Children's Books Australia
Level 17/207 Kent Street
Sydney, NSW 2000

A catalogue record of this book is available
from the British Library.

ISBN - 978 0340 91173 0 (PB)

10 9 8 7 6 5 4 3 2

Colour Reproduction by
Modern Age Repro House Ltd., Hong Kong
Printed in China

Hodder Children's Books is a division of
Hachette Children's Books.
An Hachette Livre UK Company.

One Man Went to Mow...

Hodder Children's Books

A division of Hachette Children's Books

One man went to mow,
went to mow a meadow.
One man and his dog, Spot ...

– who buried his bone –
went to mow a meadow.

Two men went to mow,
went to mow a meadow.
Two men, one man and his dog, Spot ...

- who buried his bone
and a garden gnome -
went to mow a meadow.

Three men went to mow,
went to mow a meadow.
Three men, two men,
one man and his dog, Spot ...

– who buried his bone and a garden gnome and ...

a brass trombone –

went to mow a meadow.

Four men went to mow,
went to mow a meadow.
Four men,
three men,
two men,
one man and his dog, Spot ...

– who buried his bone and a garden gnome
and a brass trombone and ...

a flat black stone -

went to mow a meadow.

Five men went to mow,
went to mow a meadow.
Five men,
four men,
three men,
two men,
one man and his dog, Spot ...

– who buried his bone
and a garden gnome and
a brass trombone and
a flat black stone and ...

a plate of scones –

went to mow a meadow.

Six men went to mow,
went to mow a meadow.
Six men,
five men,
four men,
three men,
two men,
one man
and his dog, Spot ...

– who buried his bone and a garden gnome and a brass trombone and a flat black stone and a plate of scones and ...

went to mow
a meadow.

Seven men went to mow,
went to mow a meadow.
Seven men,
six men,
five men,
four men,
three men,
two men,
one man and his dog, Spot ...

– who buried his bone and a garden
gnome and a brass trombone and a
flat black stone and a plate of scones
and Buster's bone AND ...

the Key to get
home

went to mow
a meadow.

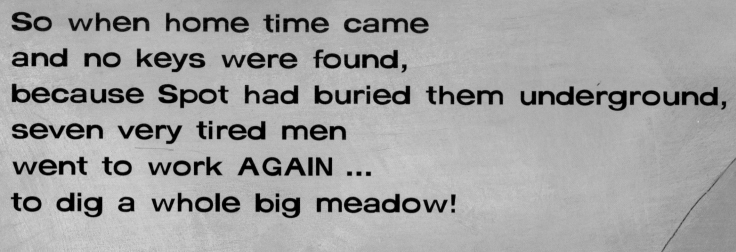

So when home time came
and no keys were found,
because Spot had buried them underground,
seven very tired men
went to work AGAIN ...
to dig a whole big meadow!

Seven men,
six men,
five men,
four men,
three men,
two men,
one man and
his dog, Spot ...

~ who buried
his bone and

a garden
gnome and

a brass
trombone and

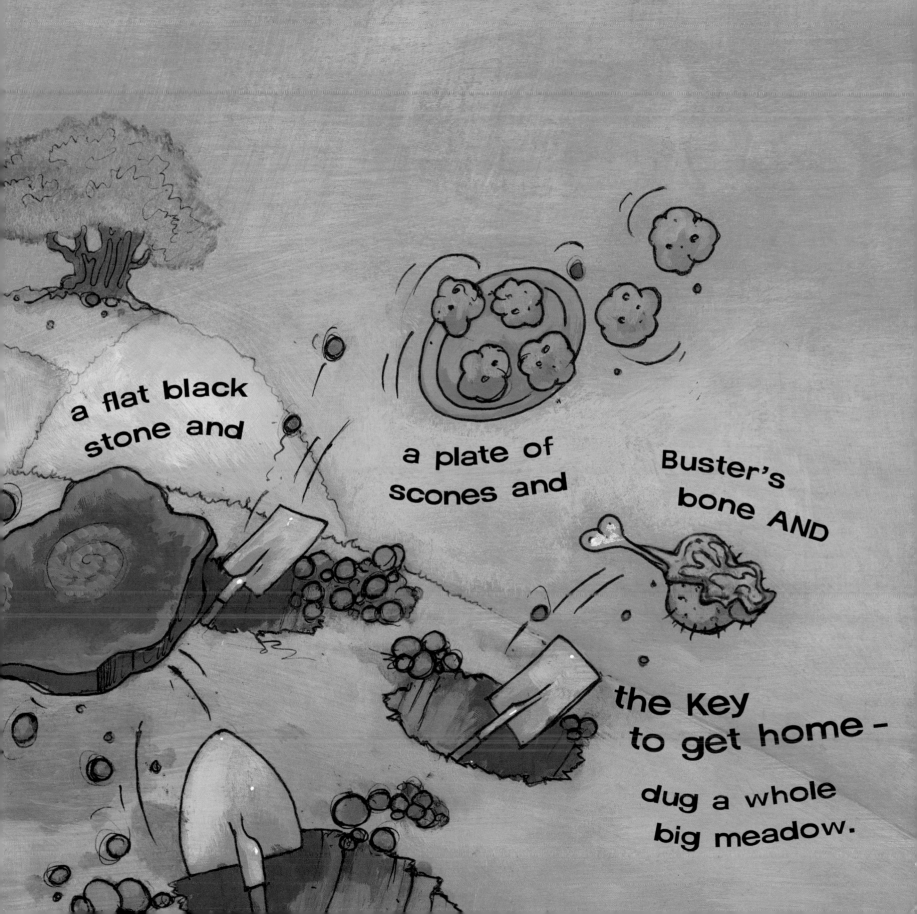

a flat black
stone and

a plate of
scones and

Buster's
bone AND

the key
to get home –

dug a whole
big meadow.